OLD DOG NEW TRICKS

BALI RAI

Barrington  Stoke

1

The first time I met Mick, I knew he was a grumpy old git. He came and rang the bell, on our first night in our new house. He lived next door, and he looked angry.

"Have you seen my budgie?" he growled. His accent was pure Leicester and really strong – when he said 'budgie', it came out like 'budgeh'.

"Your budgie?" I asked. "What – like a bird?"

"You taking the piss?" he replied.

My mum must have heard us because she joined me at the door. "What's up?" she asked.

"My budgie flew away and I thought you might have seen it," said our neighbour.

"No," said Mum. I could see she was trying not to laugh. "No budgies in our house. I think I'd notice."

The old man mumbled something under his breath.

"I'm sorry?" said Mum. "What did you say?"

"Oh, bugger off!" he snapped. Then he turned and walked away.

Mum's eyes widened and her mouth dropped open. "You can't talk to me like that!" she yelled after him.

"I know what he said," I told her. "He said we'd probably made the budgie into a curry."

Mum's expression relaxed and we burst out laughing.

The second time we met, two days later, Mick was worse. We had some of our family over for the weekend – Dad's youngest sister's lot. We were having a barbecue – the whole family was milling around the garden. My little cousin, Arjun, was messing about when he kicked my football too hard. It flew over the fence and smashed a pane of glass on Mick's greenhouse. Arjun looked shocked. He was only seven. He froze to the spot, his eyes watered, and his bottom lip trembled.

"It's OK," I told him, as my dad came over.

The fence between Mick and us was tatty and broken, and one whole panel was missing. I watched as Mick came storming out of his house, his cheeks scarlet with rage.

"You effing little moron!" he yelled across the wrecked fence.

"Oi!" I shouted back. "Don't talk to him like that – it was an accident!"

Mick ignored me and went on shouting at Arjun. "I saw you! You did it on purpose!"

"No I didn't!" Arjun protested. Then he ran to his mum, crying his eyes out.

My dad tried to calm things down. "Hi," he said to Mick. "I'm Indy Singh. What seems to be the matter?"

"That kid has just destroyed my greenhouse!" Mick yelled. He glared at my dad.

"Oh." My dad shook his head. "I'm really sorry. I'll pay for the damage."

"Stuff yer apology," Mick said. "This street was lovely before your lot started moving in."

Dad raised an eyebrow. "What you on about?" he asked. "Whose lot?"

Mick pointed to the rest of our family. "Look at you all!" he said. "Bloody infestation – that's what you are!"

"Are you being racist, mate?" Dad demanded.

Mick smirked at us. "Racist?" he said. "I'm no racist. People like you are just scum – nothing to do with yer race, mate."

That was how I met him ...

2

Later the same day, Mum, Dad and I were sitting in the kitchen. I was the youngest kid. My brother, Danny, was 16 and my sister, Ruby, had just finished Year 12 – they had both gone out.

"I just don't get racists," Dad said. "OK, some of them are ignorant. Some might be worried because they don't like change. But there's no good reason to be racist. It's just wrong."

"Like Uncle Amar and his anti-black people nonsense?" I said. Uncle Amar was my dad's brother.

"Yeah," Dad said, "like him." He looked ashamed.

"Why are you embarrassed?" Danny asked. "Ain't your fault Amar's a moron."

"I know, Harvey," my dad said. "It just winds me up."

Just then my mum walked into the kitchen carrying a load of washing. My mum is quite short, but she's proper tough. She's the one who does the telling off – Dad's too soft.

"What's up, Indy?" she asked.

"Nothing, Jas," Dad replied. "Just wound up about that racist next door. I feel angry and sad at the same time – know what I mean?"

Mum nodded.

"You two are weird," I told them. "He's a dickhead – who cares what he thinks?"

Mum gave me her look. "Language," she said. "Besides," she went on, "we should care. He's our neighbour, and we should get on. It's what Sikhs should do."

"Yeah, but we're not proper Sikhs. We're Punjabi – it's not the same thing."

The Punjab is the area of India my family first came from. It has its own language and culture, and Sikhism is the main religion. But not all Punjabis are Sikhs.

Mum shook her head. "Sikhism is a way of life," she explained. "It's not just about temples and turbans. It's about how you live and how you treat people. In that way, we are Sikhs. We believe you should show understanding to your neighbours."

"He's probably confused," Dad said. "This area's changing. Loads more non-white families – he might just be scared of change. I hate racism but I don't hate racists. I just feel sorry for them."

My mum smiled. "Well," she said, "why don't you and Harvey pop over and start again? You can take him a few samosas too – to say a proper hello."

"Good idea," said Dad.

I shook my head. "What's the point?" I protested. "He'll just shout again."

"You're 15, Harvey," Mum said. "Too old to act like a baby." She gave me another look. It meant 'Final Warning', so I shut up.

My parents gave food to all the neighbours, to say hello. Most of them were Asian like us – Sikhs, Hindus and Muslims – but there were others too. An African-Caribbean family lived three doors down, and next to them a young Polish couple. My parents soon made friends with them all – they were like that.

The paint on Mick's navy blue front door was peeling off and there was no bell. One of the house numbers had fallen off, too.

I knocked, but Mick didn't answer. I tried again but nothing happened. Dad was turning to leave when I heard a scratching sound from behind the door. It was followed by a really lazy bark. I crouched down and opened the letterbox. A wet, black snout was right in the opening. It stank.

I stepped back. "Euurrgh! It's a stinking mutt."

"I didn't know he had a dog," Dad said.

As I stood up, we heard footsteps. When the door opened, Mick glared at us. The dog tried to look at me from between Mick's legs. It was sort of grey, with big brown eyes and a shaggy coat that needed cutting. It looked friendly enough. I remembered how much I'd wanted a dog when I was in Year 7.

Mick pushed the dog back. "What do you want?" he growled.

"We want to start again," Dad said.

"Mum said to give you these," I added. I held up the bag of samosas.

Mick eyed them with a disgusted look. "What are they?"

"Samosas," I explained. "They're vegetarian, in pastry ..."

"I don't give a toss what they are!" Mick scoffed. "Get lost."

I watched Dad get angry, and then struggle to calm down. He clenched and unclenched his fists.

"You've still got the ball," I reminded Mick.

"What ball?" he asked. "The one that broke me greenhouse?"

I nodded.

"When you pay for the glass," he told me, "you can have it back."

He slammed the door in our faces. On the other side, I heard him call the dog 'Nelson'.

I looked at Dad. "Well that was a great idea," I said.

Dad shook his head. "Leave it," he said. "Sometimes old dogs can't be taught new tricks, son. They just bite anyone that tries."

3

I hadn't seen Mick for a week when Matty came over to play on my Xbox. Matty had pale skin but afro hair, because his dad was black and his mum was white. We'd been mates since nursery, and our parents were close too. So Matty knew all about the trouble we'd had with Mick.

"Mick sounds like a proper knob-head," Matty said as I shot him on the latest *Call of Duty* game. "So has he done anything since?"

"Nah – he growled at Ruby the other day but nothing else."

The Xbox was in the conservatory. It was a hot day, so we had the windows and doors open, but the blinds were drawn to stop the glare. As we started a new game, I heard soft footsteps outside.

I put my controller down, got up and looked through the blinds. The garden was empty. "Can't see no one," I said.

Matty shrugged. "Probably nothing. Seen *Crimewatch* the other day, though. They said you get more burglaries in hot weather because people go out and leave windows open."

Seconds later I heard rustling and then more footsteps, like someone was trying to tiptoe past without being heard.

"Deffo someone outside," I said. "Let's check."

Only when we went outside, we didn't find a burglar. We found Mick's nasty, skanky dog instead. Nelson.

Nelson padded over and stood in front of me. His big brown eyes were watery and his tail wagged slowly.

"I think it likes you," Matty said.

"Looks like your ex, bro."

"Shut up," Matty replied with a grin. "Best looking thing you'll ever get."

I sniffed the air. "Can you smell that?" I asked Matty.

The pong was like dirty old socks and crap.

"Them astronauts on the space station can smell that," Matty joked. "Trust!"

I looked at Nelson and waved my hand in his face. "Go on – back in yer own garden!" I told him.

Nelson didn't move. Instead, he yawned and then lay down till his head was resting on his front paws. He looked bored.

"Stupid dog!" I said.

"I like dogs," said Matty.

"Not this one," I said. "This one stinks."

Matty kneeled down and rubbed Nelson's head. "Yeah, but he's sort of cute even still."

The dog yawned again then closed his eyes. Matty was right – Nelson was cute.

I didn't hear Mick come out. I only heard his shout. "Nelson!" he yelled. "No, boy – come here!"

Mick stood in the gap between our fences, his usual angry self.

Nelson got up, shook off his coat and loped back over to Mick.

"Good dog," said Mick, crouching down and giving him a hug.

Nelson licked Mick's face and gave a little bark. They looked so close – and all of a sudden I wanted my own dog. I almost forgot about Mick being a moron, but then he stood up and glared at me.

"What are you doing with my dog?" he demanded.

I felt my face grow red even though I didn't know why. "Nothing!" I said. "He was in my garden."

Then Mick saw Matty, and something changed in his face. He looked sad for a few seconds. He turned back to me, and the scowl returned.

"I've been in your garden more times than you," he said. "The people who lived in this house were my friends. Shouldn't be allowed – pushing decent folk out ..."

"You're nuts," I told him. "We didn't push your friends out."

"Course you did," said Mick. "You and them others like you. Taking over everywhere with yer 50 kids and yer mosques ..."

"Gurdwara," I said.

"Eh?"

"Sikhs go to gurdwaras. Muslims go to mosques. We're Sikhs."

"I don't care what you are, son," he told me. "You ain't welcome, either way."

"Yeah, later Hitler ..." I said, making Matty grin.

Mick grabbed Nelson by the collar.

"What a dope," said Matty.

Nelson looked back at us as Mick dragged him inside. I felt sort of sad. I wondered why Mick was so angry. And why had he given Matty such a weird look?

4

Over the following three weeks, I saw Mick loads. He spent every day in his garden, sitting in his ratty deckchair, reading his paper and wearing the same green shorts. He hardly ever shaved and now and then he'd pick his nose and wipe the snot on his T-shirt. Nelson would sit at his side, lazing in the sunshine. He kept on winding us up – always grumpy and causing trouble. It got so bad that Mum cursed the day we moved in.

But I wasn't too bothered by Mick by then. I had worse people to bother me. Like Louis Chana.

The summer holiday that year was proper hot. I spent most of my time hanging around with my best mates, Matty and Abs. We went up the park, and into town, or just hung out on the streets. It was great, apart from Louis.

Louis was in my year, and he hated my mates and me. He had his own little crew – and they hung around by our local chippy and the off-licence next door. We saw them in the park too. They were wannabe bad boys – they thought they were all gangsta and that. Louis's family were Punjabi like mine, but they were rich. Louis lived in an eight-bedroom house, with a gated drive and a swimming pool. His old man owned a massive cash and carry, and drove a brand new Mercedes S-Class. Louis thought he was bad, but really he was just an idiot. And he was always causing trouble.

Then, one Friday, I saw Mick in the local park. And that's when things began to change ...

I was with Matty and Abs, kicking my football around. The park was packed with local kids – most of them were from my school. It was a great place to eye up the girls too, something Matty liked doing.

"Amelia and them are over there," Matty told us, nodding at the swings.

Amelia and her friends were in our year. Matty had asked Amelia out, like, ten times, but she always said no. I liked her too.

"Let's go chat to them," I suggested.

"Nah, leave it," said Abs. "She'll only diss Matty again, anyway. Besides I've got a joke for you ..." Abs was the clown in our little gang.

"Best be funny this time," said Matty. "Last one was lamer than a one-legged chicken."

Abs grinned. "What do frogs drink?" he asked.

Matty and me looked at each other.

"Go on then," I said. "What do frogs drink?"

"Croaka-cola, bruv!"

Abs started laughing and Matty groaned.

"That's bad," I said.

"Funny, though," Abs said. "Got another one too."

"Go on then, Mr Comedian ... hit us," said Matty.

Abs cleared his throat, like he was on telly or something. "Two bananas are chilling on a riverbank when this turd floats by. The turd says, 'Hey guys – come on in – the water's fine!' One banana says to the other – 'Can you believe that shit?'"

This time I groaned.

"Why were the bananas on the riverbank?" Matty asked. "It don't make no sense."

"Forget the bananas, bruv," said Abs. "The joke is about the turd ..."

"That joke is a turd," I said.

17

Just then, Matty's face fell. He pointed at the gates. Louis Chana and his mates were on bikes, winding up some younger girls.

And that's when Mick appeared, with Nelson behind him. He stopped at the gate and waited for Louis to let him past. Only Louis started mouthing off. From our distance I couldn't hear what Louis said, but I knew Mick was getting angry.

"Hey Harvey, is that your horrible neighbour?" Matty asked.

"Yeah," I replied.

I watched as Louis's mates surrounded Mick on their bikes.

One of the young girls screamed and I saw Louis get off his bike and square up to Mick. I ran towards him with Matty and Abs behind me, but before I could get there, I saw Nelson jump at Louis's mate, a lad called Wiggy. Wiggy kicked out at Nelson just as I reached them.

"Oi!" I yelled, knocking Wiggy off his bike. "Gerroff him!"

As soon as they saw us, Louis and his mates backed off. Louis glared at me. "You're dead, dickhead!" he spat.

"Yeah, yeah," I said. "You're that tough you just bullied an old man."

"None of your business, is it?"

I looked over at Mick, who was seeing to Nelson. The dog was whining in pain and I felt angry. Even though Mick was an idiot, he didn't deserve to be bullied.

"That's my neighbour," I told Louis. "If you mess with him, you mess with me."

"Ooh – hard man," Louis smirked. "We'll catch up some other time."

Louis and his mates rode out of the park, laughing and joking. I walked over to Mick.

"You OK?" I asked him.

"Bugger off!" he growled.

"But I'm just trying to help."

Mick put Nelson on his leash and turned to walk out of the park. "I don't need your help," he said. "Not yours, not anyone's."

As I watched him go, Amelia came over. "That was really brave," she said.

"I know Mick – he's my neighbour," I told her. "I was just helping."

Amelia shrugged. "Louis and his gang could have beat you up."

"Nah," I said. "No chance of that."

She grinned. "Yeah but ..." Then she winked and walked away.

I shook my head as Matty and Abs joined me. "What did Amelia say?" Matty asked.

"I dunno," I said. "She was chatting and then she just walked off. Nutter."

"I think she likes you," he told me.

"Nah, bruv," I said.

Matty just smiled. I didn't want to upset him, because I knew he really liked Amelia, but I did wonder if he was right. But even if she was into me, I wasn't gonna ask her out. Not if Matty liked her too.

I told my dad what Mick had said after I'd stood up for him. I thought he'd get angry, but he just shook his head. "I think he's lonely," he said.

"Why?" I asked.

"Because he lives on his own, and he doesn't talk to anyone," Dad told me. "I've been speaking to the neighbours. Mick's mean to all of them.

Anyway, you shouldn't be getting into fights, Harvey," he said.

"Weren't us," I protested. "It was Louis and his boys."

Dad raised an eyebrow. "You'll just have to learn to get on with Louis."

"No way," I told him. "I'd rather eat my own head."

Dad smiled. "That could be arranged."

5

That evening, as we ate, Mick started to play music so loud it sounded like it was in our own house. The kitchen cupboards were vibrating and Mum got annoyed.

"Stupid man!" she groaned.

But Mick was playing a reggae tune, and Dad smiled. "I like this song," he said. "Can't beat a bit of Bob Marley while you eat your dinner."

My sister, Ruby, was shovelling down chicken and rice like a starving pig. She had to swallow before she could speak. "Go round and tell him to get lost," she said.

"No need for that," my dad said. "We won't stoop to his level."

"If he carries on like this," said Mum, "he's getting a piece of my mind."

"What if he's a nutter?" my brother Danny asked.

"You're the nutter," Ruby told him.

But Danny wouldn't give up. "He could be," he said. "Like, what if he's one of them weirdos that kidnap kids?"

"He can take Harvey," my sister said. She spat out a bit of rice as she spoke – the smelly tramp.

After we had eaten, I helped my dad water the garden. Mick's music was still blasting out. Thing is, he was playing music we all loved. All my family hated chart music. We'd rather listen to Dad's Bob Marley CDs than some plastic pop idiot singing through a computer any day. I started thinking Mick couldn't be all bad – not if he liked such cool tunes.

"The lawn is knackered," Dad told me, like I cared. "I reckon it needs to be re-laid." He eyed the fence on Mick's side. "That looks awful, too," he said, just as Mick appeared by his back door.

"Ah," Mick said to my dad. "I wanted to speak to you."

"Mick, isn't it?" my dad replied.

"How'd you know my name?" Mick looked well suspicious.

My dad smiled. "The neighbours told me."

"Well, what you gonna do about the fence?"

My dad shook his head. "Nothing," he said. "That side is yours. I'm having some work done on our garden – can I get you a quote for yours while I'm at it?"

Mick looked angry. His face went red, his blue eyes grew wide and lines appeared on his forehead. "I don't need an effing quote!" he bellowed. "I just want the fence fixed so I don't have to look at your ugly mug!"

And Mick stormed indoors.

Two hours later, the music got louder. I was watching telly with Mum.

"I've had enough now," she said. "I don't care how good his taste in music is."

The new tune was 'Ghost Town' by The Specials. They were an old band that had re-formed, and I loved them. Dad had promised to take Danny and me to see them in concert.

When she went outside I followed, worried that Mick might be angry. My mum was fierce though – if anyone could make Mick turn his music down, she could. We walked round to Mick's front door. Mum knocked hard and I heard Nelson scratching again.

"Does the dog bite?" she asked me.

I shook my head. "No it just dribbles. Smells too."

"Takes after its owner," she whispered, as the door creaked open.

"What do you want?" Mick demanded.

"I would like you to turn the music down, please," said Mum.

Mick smiled and I saw dirty, yellow teeth. A few gaps too.

"I'd like a Ferrari," he said. "Ain't getting one though, am I?"

My mum didn't flinch. I saw her hands clench and her cheeks redden, and I knew she was getting annoyed.

"It's nearly 9 p.m.," she said. "As much as I really like The Beat, I would like some peace, please."

Mick shook his head. Nelson looked up at me, like a sad, furry bag of bones.

"Hello, Nelson," I said.

"Leave my dog alone!" Mick shouted, making me jump.

This time Mick and Nelson got a shock.

"Don't talk to my son like that!" Mum yelled. "Turn the music down!" she said. "Now!"

All of a sudden, Mick looked less angry. It was like watching a balloon lose its air. He seemed old and tired. His face relaxed and he looked away.

Mick nodded and shut the door. Moments later, the music was turned down.

That night, I couldn't sleep. It was the look on Mick's face after Mum had shouted that kept me up. He seemed to shrink and looked so much older. And even though he was a knob-head, I started to feel sorry for him.

6

The next afternoon, I called for Matty and we walked to the off-licence. It was really hot again, and the kids in our neighbourhood were hanging out on the streets. Matty had been texting Amelia's best friend, Lola, and they'd arranged to meet up.

"They're gonna be in town tomorrow," Matty told me. "Nandos and then the cinema. They said we could come too. I think I'm in there, bro."

I grinned. "I thought you liked Amelia."

"I do," Matty said. "But Lola's fit too. Think I might ask her out instead. Then you can ask Amelia."

"But I don't want to ask her out."

Matty grinned back. "You might not have a choice."

I was about to ask him what he meant, when his face dropped. "Louis and his boys," he said.

I watched Louis's crew ride up to us. Each one wore their hood up, over the top of baseball caps. It was boiling hot and they looked like idiots.

"Just ignore them," I said to Matty.

Only that was impossible. I heard shouting from the off-licence, and then Mick walked out, holding a plastic bag and grumbling. The shop owner yelled after him. "You don't bring the dog in here! I've told you before ..."

"Ah, piss off!" said Mick.

Nelson was at Mick's side. He wasn't on a leash and seemed happy about it. When he saw me, his tail started to wag.

"See?" said Matty. "That thing likes you, Harvey."

I was about to reply when Louis piped up. "Yo, old man! Why you wearing that T-shirt?"

Mick had a Bob Marley T-shirt on.

"What do you know about Bob?" Louis went on. "Old white man like you don't know shit about black people's tings, get me?"

Mick made to walk away. "Come on, Nelson!" he shouted.

Louis smirked as his mates got off their bikes.

"You best get that dog gone," he warned Mick. "Or I might have to teach it some manners."

I looked at Matty and he gave a little nod. It meant he would have my back.

I turned to Louis. "Listen, you wannabe," I said. "You touch the dog or Mick and I'm gonna batter you."

"You sticking up for him again?" Louis asked, his smirk getting wider.

Wiggy stepped closer to Matty.

"Mind your own business," I told Louis.

Mick was watching now, and his expression was soft. He looked right into my eyes and I didn't see anger or anything.

I watched Mick grab Nelson's collar and walk off. He looked back at me, like he was pleased I was standing up for him.

"Your boyfriend's going," Louis said. "Go catch him up, Harvey. Hold his hand and that ..."

Then I did something stupid. I stepped towards Louis and shoved him in the chest. He stumbled back but didn't fall over.

"You ...!"

He jumped at me, and then his boys joined in. Matty tried to help but there were five of them. I felt a couple of punches land in my side. Then Wiggy caught me in the eye.

"OW!"

I thought Matty and me would get battered but just then Mr Kosta, the chip shop owner, pulled up in his silver Mercedes. He jumped out and started shouting. Louis and his mates grabbed their bikes and rode off, laughing. I was on the ground and Mr Kosta helped me up. Matty was crouching by the steps to the off-licence and seemed OK.

"Your eye's gonna hurt in the morning, son," said Mr Kosta. "Gonna be some shiner, that."

My head was pounding and my side hurt. How was I going to explain a black eye to Mum? She'd go crazy.

"What was that about, anyway?" Mr Kosta asked. "You want me to call the police?"

As Matty joined me, I shook my head. "No," I told Mr Kosta. "No police. We ain't no snitches."

"In my day," Mr Kosta said, "those lads would get a right good kicking. But not nowadays – too many knives now. You leave it be, in case someone gets hurt bad, yeah?"

We nodded, but I knew what Matty was thinking. I was the same. Louis and his mates weren't getting away with jumping us. No way.

"What happened to your face?" Dad asked when I got home.

"Nothing," I lied. Like my black eye had just appeared from nowhere.

"Harvey?" Mum said.

"It was nothing!" I repeated.

Mum grabbed my face and looked at the bruises. "You've got a black eye," she said.

"I got into a fight," I admitted. "With Louis."

Mum's eyes widened. "Louis Chana? Why?"

I thought about telling the truth but didn't. I don't know why. "We just don't get on," I said. "He had a go at me, and I pushed him and –"

"That's not right!" Mum snapped. "I'm going to call his parents!"

Before I could stop her, she was off. I groaned. Louis was going to love that – my mum snitching to his parents.

"I can hear Mick's music again," I said, desperate to change the subject.

Dad nodded. "Yeah – sounds all right to me."

"It's loud," I said.

"Jimi Hendrix should be played loud," Dad told me. "Maybe Mick has got friends after all. Sounds like a party."

But when I went into the garden to get away from Mum's phone call, I saw Mick through his dirty windows. He was alone, sitting in a ratty old armchair, pretending to play a guitar. A can of lager sat on one of the chair arms, and Nelson was at his feet.

Mick saw me watching him. He held the can of lager up and winked. I saw his mouth moving, but didn't hear what he said. Maybe he was thanking me for standing up to Louis. I hoped so – something had to make the bruises worth it. Then he went back to playing air-guitar.

7

On Saturday morning, we were all at the Sikh temple – the gurdwara. Danny and Ruby were outside in the sunshine, while I ended up in the kitchen, helping Mum. I was gutted because I couldn't meet Matty in town. I imagined him surrounded by Amelia and her friends – living it up – and I got jealous. I couldn't believe I was stuck in the temple, especially when Louis Chana and his family turned up. When Louis saw my black eye, he smirked and shook his head. I wanted to punch him, which is why Mum made me help out.

We were preparing food with three of my aunts. Seven other women were making chapattis over a huge hotplate. They were all family too. My uncle Amar was walking around, showing people what to do. Not helping, Mum said – just being a pain in the bum. When Amar saw me, he half smiled.

"Hello Harvind," Amar said. Harvind is my real name, but most people call me Harvey. People I like, that is. "You're getting bigger," he said to me.

I wanted to ask what he'd been expecting. Like, 'Do people get smaller?' But I knew Mum would go mad, so I just smiled.

"You should be outside. Not in here, doing women's work. Tell your sister to come and help."

I waited for Mum to react but she didn't. She just sighed. "Ruby isn't any use in a kitchen," she said.

"But she's 18," Amar pointed out. "Surely she can make food by now?"

My mum had a knife to slice the tomatoes. Her fingers gripped it harder. Uncle Amar gave a sly little smile. He knew he was winding Mum up.

"I like her to concentrate on her education," Mum said. "She can learn to cook later."

"But when she gets married," he continued, "how will she cook for her husband?"

Mum's knuckles went white and her face grew pink. "Perhaps," she said through gritted teeth, "her husband will cook for her!"

Uncle Amar started to laugh. "That is a white person's thing to say," he replied. "You are not white."

Thankfully, my dad's sister Mandy appeared before mum could draw blood. "Amar," Mandy said, "you're needed in the main hall."

Amar went off and Aunt Mandy apologised to my mum. "He doesn't mean any harm," she added. "He's just a bit old-school, that's all."

Mum waited till my aunt had walked away too and then she whispered, "I'll do him harm in a minute!"

"He's a dick," I said.

Mum glared at me. "He's still your uncle, Harvey. You talk about him with respect!"

I rolled my eyes and went outside, wondering why parents were so freaky. Why tell me to respect my uncle, when they hated him?

A couple of hours later, I had my run-in with Louis. I knew it would happen. Sikhs make a meal at the temple. It's called a 'langar' and anyone can eat it. You don't even have to be Sikh. All day long, they cook loads of stuff and brew gallons of spicy tea too. The women were already making food for the evening when I decided to eat something. I got a steel tray, with six little sections to it, and lined up. A group of men stood behind huge pots of curry and they dished out what everyone wanted. I had lentil curry and two chapattis, and ate standing at a table. Danny and Ruby joined me, followed by loads of my cousins.

"Look who's over there ..." said Danny.

I turned round, expecting to see another uncle or something. My family is huge. But it wasn't family. It was Louis, standing at a table, glaring at me. Two other lads stood with him, both about my brother's age.

"You just gonna let him do that?" asked Danny. He was trying to wind me up, and it was working.

"Shut up," I said.

"Man gave you a beating, bro," Danny went on. "And now look at him. Standing there, giving it the big one."

"It wasn't him who punched me," I said. "It was his mate."

"Still his crew, though," Danny replied.

My brother was a wind-up merchant – and good at it. I started to clench and unclench my fists.

"Who's he with?" I asked.

"Them two?" Danny said. "They're his cousins. They ain't nothing. I got your back."

All of a sudden I snapped. I stormed over to Louis. When he realised I was coming for him, he stopped looking so cool. I saw the fear in his face. He looked around, but the lads with him backed off. He was on his own.

"Yeah?" he said, trying to act hard.

Thing is, he wasn't wearing his gangsta clothes in the gurdwara. His bad boy act didn't work in there.

"Let's see how brave you are now," I said. "When your boys ain't with you."

"What?" he said. "You wanna fight me in here, blood? Disrespect the religion?"

I shook my head. "No," I told him. "Let's go outside. There's a factory yard over the road. In there ..."

"I ain't going nowhere," he replied. "You've probably got an ambush ready, innit. You think I'm stupid?"

I smiled at him. "An ambush?" I asked. "You watch too many films, Louis."

"You wanna say summat," he went on. "Say it here. Or maybe you wanna get your mum to help you out? She told my mum I hit you, when I didn't. Can't you fight your own battles, bro?"

I felt myself getting angrier. Louis wasn't going to man up and come outside, and I couldn't batter him inside. That would be bad. So instead, I grabbed Louis's tray of curry and tipped it over him.

"What you doing, you dickhead?" he shouted.

"Sorry," I said. "It was an accident."

I walked away.

"You're gonna have an accident when I'm cleaned up!" warned Louis.

But Louis didn't do anything. I spent the rest of the day getting bored. Then, just as the evening meal started, my dad had a massive bust-up with Uncle Amar.

It started because two homeless men came in to eat. They wore dirty, baggy clothes and were really smelly. They lined up, got their food, and took it to the far end of the main hall. After a few minutes, one of the temple's organisers approached them. I was too far away to hear, but I could see they were having a row. The homeless men looked embarrassed and the other guy was pointing at them with his finger.

I was with Dad and Danny, and Uncle Amar came over.

"Look at those tramps!" he said. "They can't come in here!"

"That's not very Sikh, is it?" said my dad.

Uncle Amar pulled a face. "We don't allow those people to eat here," he said. "They are nothing but scroungers."

My dad got really furious. "Shut up, Amar!" he shouted, as everyone in the dining hall stopped to stare. "You don't talk about people that way," Dad went on. "They have as much right to eat here as you. You're supposed to be a Sikh – or at least behave like a Sikh. Learn what that means!"

"Maybe they should get jobs instead of scrounging."

Then my dad used a very bad word. Uncle Amar smirked.

"Typical gorah," he said, using the Punjabi word for white man.

"You thick, judgemental, bigoted moron!" Dad yelled. "They aren't scroungers. They're just skint. And we're supposed to help people like that – not call them names."

Dad took my arm and we walked out. He was fuming. When my mum came to check on us, Dad told her what had happened.

"OK," said Mum. "Let me get the other two."

And then we left.

Later that evening, we ordered pizza and fried chicken, and went and pigged out in the garden. Dad explained why he'd been so angry.

"Sikhs have a duty to help people in need," he told me. "The gurdwara is open to anyone who isn't drunk or doesn't offend people. It's like a social club for the community."

"Like them old people who sit around chatting all day?"

Dad nodded. "Yes," he said. "Imagine how lonely those old folk would be, stuck at home all day. The temple gives them something to look forward to. It should be a place for everyone in the community."

I thought of Mick – sitting in his crappy old chair, with his cheap lager and his loud music. I wondered if he was lonely too. We were lucky because our family was big. We had each other. I'd never seen Mick with anyone except Nelson.

Dad grabbed another chicken wing, and Danny and Ruby argued over the slice of pizza with the most pepperoni on it. Ruby won, after she pushed Danny off his chair. Mum went mad at them. I sat and wondered about Mick some more.

8

Two days later I was waiting for Matty to come round. It was morning and I was having a kick-about with my spare football. Mick was sunbathing in his garden. He still hadn't given my first ball back. When he noticed me, he sort of half-nodded.

"You OK, mate?" I said.

Mick gave me a funny look. "You talking to me?" he asked.

I kicked the ball away and nodded. "No one else in your garden. Where's Nelson?" I added.

"None of your business," he said.

This time, instead of getting annoyed, I smiled. Mick seemed shocked.

"Why are you so miserable?" I asked.

He shrugged. "Who says I'm miserable?"

"Everyone," I told him. "All the neighbours. They say you don't talk to anyone."

"Used to talk to Francis," he said.

"Who?"

"The man you bought your house from. Me and Franny used to go down the pub most nights. He were a good un, were Franny." He looked over his overgrown garden. "Things were different back then."

I was puzzled. "But we only moved in a few weeks ago," I said. "And you must know where Franny is. Why don't you visit him?"

Mick chuckled. "Can you get return tickets to wherever dead people go?"

"You mean heaven?" I asked.

"If you believe in that," he said. "Franny died about two year ago. It were his kids that sold the house."

"Oh," I said. "Sorry, mate."

Mick shrugged again, and I saw sadness in his eyes. His kitchen door was open, and Nelson came out. When he saw me, the dog wagged his tail.

"I think Nelson likes me," I said, to change the subject.

"Doubt it," Mick said. "He don't like the smell of curry."

Again, I didn't get wound up. I thought Mick was trying to test me.

"If I smell of curry, you smell of lager and chips," I said.

"Chips?" he said. "What the flippin' heck you on about?"

"You said curry because you think that's all Asian people eat. So I picked a typical English food ... chips."

Mick smiled. Well, sort of. "Chips weren't invented in England," he told me. "That were the Belgians or the French or summat."

"So what – you eat them so you smell of chips then."

"Ain't the same, is it?" he said. "When your mum is cooking, the smell comes right into my house."

Nelson lay down and rested his head on my foot.

"Why are you so racist?" I asked.

Mick shook his head. "I'm not," he said. "I just don't like the way this area's changed. Used to be lovely."

"It still is, Mick," I replied. "Everyone's all chilled out and people are friendly."

"Apart from your mates in the park," he said. "That's some shiner, by the way."

I touched my right eye. The bruise was purple now. "I got this because I was defending you," I said.

"Didn't ask you to," he said. "I were just minding my own business."

"Them lads are fools," I said. "They go to my school."

"They should ship 'em out to Iraq," he grunted. "Bloody layabouts. That wouldn't have happened ten years ago."

I looked up at his house – the grimy windows, with their rotten frames, and the tatty curtains. Part of the gutter had fallen down, and there were loads of tiles missing from his roof.

"Where are your kids?" I asked.

Mick didn't face me. "Ain't got none," he said, but I knew he was lying. I could just tell.

"You're all right, mate," I said. "Like, a bit weird, but not as nasty as I thought."

He turned to me, looking confused. "Why should I care what you think of me?" he asked.

"Everyone cares," I told him. "Everyone needs friends."

"You don't know anything about me, lad!" he snapped.

"I know you like cool music," I said. "Jimi Hendrix, Bob Marley, The Specials – I love all of those."

He smiled again – only this time it was warm. "What the hell does a sprat like you know about them people?" he asked. "You weren't even born when they were around."

"Not The Specials," I said. "They're back. Dad's gonna get me tickets to see them."

"Me and Franny saw 'em in Coventry, back in 1979. They were magic!" Mick said.

"Man – you're old," I said. "Like proper old."

Mick nodded. "I'd rather be old than stuck growing up now," he said. "All them computers and bloody smart phones. Your generation will go blind, I'm telling yer."

"That's what Dad says, too," I told him.

"Too many immigrants an' all," Mick added. "Like – half of this city don't even look English."

"Do I look English?" I asked him.

"No mate," he said. "You do not."

"But if you were blind, Mick, and heard me speak," I said. "Would I sound English then?"

He screwed up his face. "Well, yeah."

"Most of those non-white people are like me and Matty," I said.

"Who's Matty?"

"My mate from the other day?"

Mick nodded. "That half-caste lad ..."

"You don't say that any more," I told him. "It's offensive. He's mixed-race."

"He's bloody half-caste, son, and I'm not being offensive."

I shook my head, thinking about all the music Mick liked. "How can you be that racist and listen to Bob Marley?" I asked.

"Bob Marley ain't in my garden asking stupid questions, is he?"

I realised he was messing with me. I looked at Nelson, got a whiff of his dirty coat, and had an idea.

"Can I take Nelson over to mine for a bit?" I asked.

Mick eyed me. "Why?"

"Just to play ball and that," I replied. "Might even shower him with the hose. He stinks ..."

Mick nodded. "If you like. There's dog shampoo under the sink in the kitchen. Help yourself, but don't be thieving me stuff ..."

He winked at me and closed his eyes. "I know what you Arabs are like ..."

Mick's kitchen was a total mess. It was old-fashioned and the cooker sat on its own, covered in grease. The sink under the window was full of dirty dishes. I saw mould floating in the water. The floor was sticky and grimy, and it smelled terrible.

No wonder Mick was miserable. Imagine living in this place. I should have taken the shampoo and left right away, but something made me stay. I walked into the hallway and into his lounge. It was even worse than the kitchen. There were cans of lager and open tins of dog food all over the floor.

I searched the walls and shelves for pictures, wondering if Mick had family, but there was nothing. Just one poster, of a band called The Jam.

"You got lost in there, lad?" I heard him shout from the garden.

I rushed back out with the shampoo. "Took a while to find it," I lied.

Mick nodded, closed his eyes again and started snoring in seconds. I looked at Nelson.

"Come on then, you stinker," I said.

Nelson stood, wagged his tail and farted.

9

Nelson followed me eagerly. I wondered if he was hungry, and remembered a leftover sandwich in our fridge. I went and got it, and when Nelson smelled the ham, he jumped up and wagged his tail. I broke a bit off and fed it to him. His tongue was wet and rough against my hand, but I didn't care. He was cool.

"Good boy!" I said.

I took a quick glance over the fence at Mick, but he was fast asleep.

Just then Danny came into the garden. "What's that dog doing here?" he asked.

"SHHHH!!!" I snapped. "You'll wake Mick up!"

Danny shrugged. "So? Why you feeding that mutt, anyway?"

I patted Nelson before I replied. "He was hungry," I said. "He wants to be friends. Look how cute he is ..."

Danny grinned. "It looks like a giant, dirty rat," he said. "I bet your hand is covered in germs."

I grabbed Nelson's collar and we walked to the tall trees at the back of the garden. Nelson ran in and out of the trunks, chased his tail and yelped. When at last he got bored, he sat down and wagged his tail again.

"I'm gonna wash him," I said to Danny.

"What – in our bathroom?" Danny screwed up his nose. "Mum'll batter you, mate."

"Not the bath," I said. "I ain't stupid. I'm gonna use the hose."

Then Ruby appeared on the patio, holding a plate of toast. "You're gonna do what?" she asked.

"Wash Nelson," I said.

She rolled her eyes. "You're weird. Like, I thought you didn't like Mr Racist next door?"

"Nah," I said. "He's OK really – just a bit mad, that's all."

"Well, you best be careful," she warned. "Get that water near me and you're dead."

"Scared you might get clean?" Danny joked.

"I'll clean them manky teeth out of your mouth in a minute," Ruby warned. "Cheeky sod."

Our hose had a spray gun attached, and I set it on 'shower'. I called Nelson to me and stood him on the lawn. Then I squeezed the trigger and soaked him. He loved it – running round and round and barking like crazy. His grey coat was long and tangled and when he shook the water off, it went everywhere.

"Harvey!" Ruby screamed.

I looked up and saw splashes of water by her feet.

"Sorry," I said, even though I wasn't really bothered.

Once Nelson was dripping wet, I sprayed the shampoo all over him. I was careful not to go near his eyes or mouth. But when I tried to grab him to rub the soap in, he ran off.

"Nelson!" I yelled, but he didn't listen.

Instead, he ran straight for Ruby, who panicked. "Get away!" she shrieked.

Nelson ignored her and started to lick her leg.

"Harvey!" Ruby yelled. She stood on her chair to get away.

I started laughing so much that my eyes watered.

I let her stew before I went over and dragged the dog away.

Nelson looked so happy as I rubbed shampoo into his coat and then washed it off. Loads of hair came away too, and the water was grimy, but I didn't care. I washed him twice before I was done. And I was soaked, too. When my mum came out, she shook her head and told me to have a shower.

"What's his dog doing here?" she asked me.

"I did what you said," I told her. "I'm making an effort with our neighbour."

"Dog's quite cute, isn't he?" Mum said.

I smiled and watched Nelson shake water from his coat again.

When Matty came by, I took Nelson back to Mick.

"He looks good," Mick said. "Like new."

"Thanks for letting me play with him," I said.

"I suppose I should thank you for cleaning him up," said Mick.

"It's OK," I replied. "You don't have to thank me."

Mick told me to hang on. He went in and came back with my ball. "There you go," he said, as he handed it to me. "No use to me anyway."

"You're a funny old man," I told him.

"You're a funny lad," said Mick.

Later on, Matty and me went to the park. We found Abs talking to Amelia and Lola about some pop band. When they saw us, Lola smiled.

"Hey, Matty!" she called.

Matty smiled back and looked at me. "I asked her out," he told me, making sure Lola didn't hear. "On Saturday. We're going to the cinema again later. If you want to ask Amelia, I won't mind."

We walked over to join them. Amelia asked me if I wanted to go to the cinema too. I shook my head.

"Not tonight," I said.

Matty glared at me, and Abs just shook his head. Amelia's face fell and she looked a bit annoyed. I thought fast. My parents were having a party the next day. I was going to ask my mates along anyway, so I asked Amelia too. Her face lit up.

"Yeah!" she said. "That would be cool!"

"Great," I said.

Matty shook his head as we walked home. "You nearly blew that," he said. "Lucky for you, me and Abs were about. You need some serious help with your technique."

"What technique?"

"Your woman skills," said Abs.

"You sure you can't come tonight?" Matty asked.

"Nah," I said. "It's Monday – I have to help Mum make dinner on Mondays. Unless you want to ask her for me?"

Matty shook his head again. "No way, bruv," he said. "Your mum is scary."

Abs started grinning. "I've got a joke about mums," he said. "Your momma is so stupid she got run over by a parked car!"

Matty and me looked at each other.

"Abs!"

Then we fell silent. I thought about Amelia and Mick, and how fast things can change. I didn't realise it then, but things were about to change again.

10

My parents' party was the next day. They invited most of their mates and some of the neighbours too. I stayed to help, but Ruby went out and Danny had a sleepover at his best mate's. The house was busy from early evening, and Dad took control of the barbecue. I helped him cook sausages and homemade burgers until I got too hot.

My friends came early and sat down by the trees. Amelia was wearing a yellow dress and she looked amazing. When Dad saw her, he turned to me and smiled.

"Is that your girl?" he asked.

"No," I replied. "At least, I don't think so."

Dad shook his head. "You don't think so?" he asked. "The way she smiled at you, you'd better ask her out!"

Later on, as I was chilling with my mates, Dad's best friend Jeff came over. "You OK, Harvey?" Jeff asked, as he chewed on a hotdog slathered in mustard and ketchup.

"Yeah," I said, and introduced him to everyone.

I love Uncle Jeff – he's fun and he listens to me. But he was also the reason my dad fell out with Uncle Amar. Jeff was black, and my uncle didn't like him.

"Nice eye," Jeff said. "You been fighting?"

I explained what had happened with Louis's gang and why. Uncle Jeff nodded.

I hadn't told my dad the real reason for my fight with Louis. I looked over at him now, in his Bob Marley apron, chatting to my mum's best friend and not watching the sausages.

"I got jumped because I was helping the man next door," I said.

"The racist bloke? Your dad told me about him," he said. "Man sounds like an idiot."

"He's not that bad," I told him. "I think he's just lonely. He is a bit racist. But it doesn't help when people like Louis are mean to him. And, like, he listens to Bob Marley and Jimi Hendrix – so he can't be that racist, can he?"

As I said it, I had an idea. Uncle Jeff went off to help dad with the barbecue and I told Amelia I was going round to Mick's to invite him too.

"Do you wanna come with me?" I asked.

"Yeah," she said, with a grin. "It can be our first date."

As she stood up, Matty winked at me. Maybe Amelia did like me. Thing is, I didn't get a chance to think about that properly, because Nelson appeared at the gap in the fence. He looked at me and whined. Then he looked back at Mick's house.

"Nelson?" I said. "What's up boy?"

Nelson whined some more.

"He's telling you something," Amelia said.

Amelia followed me through the gap in the fence. Mick's back door was open but there was no sign of him.

"That's weird," I said. "He's normally in the garden when the door's open."

"Maybe he's just popped inside?" said Amelia. "Like, to the bathroom or something?"

Nelson led us to the door. I knocked but got no reply. "Mick?"

When he didn't respond, I thought about leaving it. But then Amelia grabbed my hand. The shock made me jump.

"Can you hear that?" she said. "The dog is whimpering."

I studied Nelson. His eyes were watery and downcast.

"Something's wrong," I said. "I think we should go in."

I followed Nelson into the living room and I saw why he was so upset. Mick had fallen over. He was lying on the nasty carpet with his eyes closed. "Mick?" I shouted. "Mick – can you hear me?"

I wanted to check him but I was scared. I didn't want to do anything wrong.

"Is he dead?" Amelia asked. She grabbed my hand again and squeezed really hard. She looked like she was going to cry.

I shook my head. "I dunno. Come on – let's get help!"

We ran back to mine and I saw my mum.

"MUM!" I shouted. "MUM! It's Mick," I babbled. "I think he's hurt!"

Mum grabbed her best friend, Juliet, who was a doctor. Juliet still had a chicken wing in her hand as I led them through the fence and into the house.

There was Mick, lying on the grimy carpet. But this time his eyes opened. His face was so pale – like the skin had been bleached. He was clutching his chest.

"We're here now," said Juliet. "Just take it easy ..."

Nelson sat down next to me. He looked really upset.

"It's OK, boy," I told him. "Mick will be fine."

Mum put her hand on my shoulder. "Take Amelia and Nelson outside," she said.

I wanted to stay but I could see she knew best. Juliet was already on the phone, talking to the emergency services. I could tell by her face that Mick was in serious trouble. I started to wonder if he would die.

Juliet and Dad went with Mick in the ambulance. The guests all began to leave, and I saw my friends off.

"Call me," Amelia said. "Let me know how Mick is."

"I will."

"And Harvey?"

I looked at her.

"That was a weird first date," she said.

It was a joke, but she wasn't smiling. I think she was just trying to make me feel better.

When everyone had left, I brought Nelson round to ours. He sat down in the kitchen and whined.

I sat up for ages but my dad didn't come back. In the end, I took Nelson up to my room and lay there trying to get some sleep.

11

Dad took me to see Mick two days later. He was lying in bed, staring into space. He had his own room, which was too warm. There were white pads attached to his chest. A machine sat next to his bed, bleeping every few seconds.

"Hi Mick!" I said.

He grunted at me, and then nodded. His skin was almost grey and he had a grizzly layer of stubble on his face. He looked so different to the angry man I first met. He looked helpless.

I told him about Nelson and how I'd walked him, twice each day. Mick didn't reply because he couldn't speak properly. His eyes were moist and he tried to lift an arm.

"What's the matter?" I whispered to my dad.

"He's not had his operation yet," Dad whispered back.

Mick had suffered a cardiac arrest – according to my mum – a heart attack. It was a bad one too, and he was lucky that Amelia and me found him when we did.

"He's got no energy and he can't move very well," Dad said.

I asked Mick where his family was, but he turned his eyes away.

"I can contact them, if you like," I said. "I'm sure they'd want to be here."

When Mick looked back, he'd shed a few tears. He shook his head. "NO," he managed to say in a croak.

I didn't want to upset him, so I stopped asking.

A nurse walked in and looked at his chart.

"The doctor is coming to see him in a moment, about his operation," she told my dad.

Dad looked at Mick. "Do you want me to stay?" he asked. Mick nodded.

"My son, Harvey, found him," Dad told the nurse. He sounded really proud.

The nurse smiled at me. She had shiny, dark skin and spoke with an African accent. She was very pretty.

"You saved his life," she told me. "You're a hero."

I didn't see Mick again until after his operation. I spent all that time looking after Nelson, chilling with my mates or going into town with Amelia. We'd started seeing each other properly a few days after we found Mick. I was really happy – Amelia was loads of fun. She was even happy to walk Nelson with me, and she offered to help clean Mick's house as a surprise for him.

I shrugged. "We should ask him first," I said.

"But that won't be a surprise," she protested.

"Let me ask my mum."

Mum wasn't convinced. "I'm not sure Mick would want you to go through his stuff," she said.

"But we'd just get rid of rubbish," I told her. "We won't take anything else."

"I dunno," she said. "If it was me ..."

"You could supervise us," I pleaded. "You're on holiday, aren't you?"

"Ye-e-s," Mum said. "Holiday – which means I don't want to be cleaning out Mick's house. I've got enough to do around here."

"Well then me and Amelia will do it."

Mum thought about it. "OK," she said at last. "I guess when he's allowed to come home – if he's allowed to come home – he'll have nurses visiting him, and I don't think he'd like them to see the state of his house. But don't break anything and don't look at his personal stuff. When are you going to do it?" Mum asked.

"Tomorrow," I told her. "After I've taken Nelson for his walk."

Mum nodded. "Talking of which," she said, looking at her watch, "isn't he due a walk now?"

I took Nelson to the park, but he wasn't his usual self. I found a stick. Normally, he'd growl and chew on it, and wag his tail. But today he just sat and stared over the park.

On the way back, Louis Chana and Wiggy appeared.

"Oi – dickhead!" said Louis, in his fake gangsta voice. "You got anything to say now?"

Louis was in my face, with Wiggy behind him. I tried to walk on. But Wiggy grabbed me from behind and Louis took hold of my top. Nelson whined.

"You think you're hard, bro?" Louis snarled.

"Man was giving it large in the temple, innit?" said Wiggy.

I realised that I was going to get battered, but then Nelson went mad. He gave a sudden growl, much angrier than I'd ever heard him before. Louis backed off, his eyes wide.

"Best call that dog off!" he said, but his voice was shaking. Nelson turned and snarled at Wiggy, who let go too. When Wiggy kicked out, Nelson grabbed his leg and shook it.

"GERROFF ME!" Wiggy screamed, like a little kid.

I pulled Nelson away, and he let go. Wiggy held his leg and started to blubber.

Louis had moved away by then. I grabbed Nelson's collar and undid the leash. Nelson was raring up, trying to get at Louis.

"What you doing, Harvey?" Louis asked. The fear was obvious in his voice. "You best not set that ..."

He didn't finish his sentence. Instead he ran off up the road, past my house, as Nelson gave chase. He was wailing and bawling, and begging me to call Nelson off. He just ran and ran. I laughed so much, tears came to my eyes. I knew Nelson wouldn't hurt him.

At last I called Nelson off. The dog stopped in his tracks and trotted back over to me. Louis was long gone. I grinned and led Nelson into my house.

"Good dog!" I told him. "We should change your name to Gangsta Killer!"

12

Amelia and I spent the morning cleaning Mick's living room. I grabbed some black bags and other stuff from ours. Amelia insisted on wearing rubber gloves, and I couldn't blame her. It was a minging job. We filled four bags, and sprayed everything with anti-bacterial spray. It made a huge difference – like it was a new room, almost.

I usually hated doing stuff like this, but it was OK with Amelia there.

I told her about my latest run-in with Louis and Wiggy.

"What if they call the police?" she said. "Nelson could get taken away."

I shook my head. "That won't happen. They won't admit to being chased off by Nelson. They'll be way too embarrassed."

I'd have to face Louis and his mates at school next week, but I didn't care. With any luck, they'd think twice about picking on me now.

We did the bedroom in the afternoon. The amount of stuff was crazy. We filled three bags with clothes and belongings, and six bags with rubbish.

By late evening, we were ready to make a start on Mick's kitchen. The first thing we found in there was a big cardboard box, hidden underneath a pile of newspapers under the table. It was really heavy, but I managed to pull it out. I opened the box and saw photo frames and cards and a stack of unopened letters. They were all addressed to 'Mick Havelock'.

"Hey," I said to Amelia. "Look at this."

"We shouldn't be looking at his stuff," she said, sounding like my mum.

"I wasn't," I said. "I thought it was more rubbish. Look – these letters have his full name on."

Amelia came over as I put the letters to one side and pulled out some photos. Mick looked so young in them, and he was with a really beautiful woman. In one, they were outside a church – a wedding photo. Mick had a wife. I found others, of a baby, then a little girl, and finally a woman. Mick's daughter, I realised.

In the last one, Mick was standing next to a gravestone, holding hands with his daughter. His eyes looked puffy, like he'd been crying. When I looked closer, the stone read 'In Loving Memory of Diane Havelock – Wife & Mother'. I felt a lump in my throat.

"Wow," said Amelia. "This is like seeing his whole life ... It must be his box of precious things – we shouldn't be looking at it."

"I didn't know any of this," I said. "He said he didn't have kids. I knew he was lying."

Amelia gave me a puzzled look. "But why would he lie?"

"I dunno," I said. "Maybe we could find out?" I nodded at the box.

"What if he goes mad?" Amelia asked. "Like, because we looked at his things?"

"I'm sure his family would want to know if he's ill. Maybe we can help him?" I said. "Get in touch with his children?"

Amelia thought about what I was saying. In the end, she nodded.

I started with a letter. It was one of many, all addressed in the same handwriting. I knew that opening someone else's mail was wrong. But I just wanted to know about Mick's children. Surely they'd want to see him? I thought about the picture in the box. I wondered what his wife had been like. Had Mick been a nicer, happier man when she was alive? He'd looked happy in a lot of the photos.

I stared at the envelope for ages before I opened it. There was an address at the top. It was from a lady called Jenny Warren, and started with the words 'Dear Dad'. So Jenny was Mick's daughter.

Amelia and me read all of it. Jenny had sent her dad loads of letters, and he'd never replied. He had two grandchildren, Rosie and Luca, who were around my age. But Mick had never met them. Mick didn't like Jenny's husband, Anthony. And we knew why from the letter.

'Can't you live and let live, Dad? PLEASE??? Anthony and the kids are human beings, just like you. Why can't you see past skin colour? What happened to my amazing dad?'

"He really is a racist, isn't he?" Amelia said.

"Looks like it," I said. "It's so sad. It's clear Jenny loves him."

We were so wrapped up in it all, we didn't notice my mum at the door.

"What are you two doing?" she demanded.

"Er ..." I looked at the letter in my hands, and Amelia went bright red.

A little while later, I was on the brown leather sofa in our house, sulking. My mum and dad looked unimpressed. I was waiting for a full-on lecture. Amelia had gone home and Nelson was asleep in the kitchen.

"We'll start," said Mum, "with why you did it."

"I wanted to know if Mick had a family," I told them. "To help him."

Mum shook her head. "You don't help by stealing his letters. They're private, Harvey."

I shook my head. "I didn't steal them. I just looked at them."

Mum wasn't having it. "They weren't opened," she said. "And you opened them – without Mick's permission. That is stealing."

"Only one," I protested. "And it was because I was worried!"

"Do you know it's against the law?" asked Mum. "To open someone else's mail?"

I nodded. "But ..." I began.

"Mick's problems with his family are private," Mum told me. Her voice was calmer now.

"I know that – but he's unhappy," I mumbled.

"That's his business."

"But what if he dies?" I asked, beginning to get upset.

Mum looked at Dad. He shrugged.

"Then we'll deal with that," she said.

"But he's got a child!" I blurted out. "Grandkids too!"

Mum gave me a weird look. "Did you say family?"

"Yeah," I said. "A daughter, who's old, like you two. And grandkids, from Jenny. Jenny's been trying to get in touch, but Mick didn't reply. He didn't even read the letters. How can we let Mick die without telling his daughter?"

Dad put his hand on my shoulder. "No one knows if he'll die," he said. "With any luck he'll be fine once his heart is fixed."

"What good is his heart when his life is broken?" I asked.

My parents exchanged glances again, and then Dad grinned. "You're like a baby Buddha, sometimes," he told me.

"Huh?" I said.

"Buddha," said Mum. "Like a wise man."

"Yeah," said Dad. "Sometimes, you say stuff that puts adults to shame."

I had no idea what he was banging on about, so I just told them more.

"Jenny married a man called Anthony Warren," I said. "Mick didn't like him. I think Anthony's black."

"Anthony Warren ..." said Mum. "You know that name, Indy?"

Dad thought for a while, and then he nodded. "Yeah," he said, "if it's the same one."

"It says in the letter that Jenny lives in Ashby," I said, getting excited. "That's near Twycross Zoo, isn't it? So you'll really help find Jenny?" I asked.

Mum smiled at me. "I can't see what harm it'll do. But you're still in trouble."

"I don't care," I said. "If I can help Mick, I'll be happy."

"You like him, don't you?" Mum said.

"He's OK, I guess," I told her. "He's just an old dog."

When she looked confused, I glanced at Dad and grinned.

13

Mick had his operation the next week. Dad went to see him the following day, and I hurried back from school to find out how Mick was.

"Mick's fine. Uncle Jeff is coming round," Dad said.

"Why?"

Dad grinned. "It's a surprise," he told me, annoyingly.

By the time Uncle Jeff arrived, I was going crazy. I wanted to know what the surprise was. And how did it connect to Mick?

"Uncle Jeff knows Anthony Warren," Dad told me.

"He's my cousin," said Jeff.

My eyes nearly popped out of my head. How mad was that?

"So you know Mick's daughter, too?"

Jeff nodded. "Sort of," he said. "Me and Anthony aren't close, but I went to their wedding."

"So you can call him," I said.

Dad grinned at me. "We already have. Jenny's meeting us at the hospital – in an hour."

I was really excited about meeting Mick's family. I kept thinking how happy Mick would be.

"Don't get your hopes up," Dad said, as we waited by the hospital entrance. "We can't control how Mick will react."

"Didn't you tell him?"

Dad shook his head.

"But what if he gets angry?" I asked. "He might get worse."

"Yes, I know," Dad said. "So I'm going in first, to break it to him. If he's OK, Jenny will see him. If not, then there's nothing else we can do."

If Mick went mad because we contacted his daughter, I'd be gutted.

Dad could see what I was thinking. "You tried, Harvey," he told me. "You're a star for doing this much. Most lads would just ignore Mick's troubles."

We were still waiting in the hospital entrance when Mick's daughter arrived.

"Jenny," said Uncle Jeff, and gave her a hug.

Jenny smiled at me. "You must be Harvey," she said.

I nodded, but I was too shy to reply.

As she started to thank me for saving her dad's life, I felt myself blush. I didn't know what to say. Then Jenny started crying, and I felt bad.

"You're a fantastic young man," she told me. "Just great!"

I was so embarrassed that I turned away, and I saw my dad grinning at me.

"Well, say something," he told me.

I shrugged. "Nelson helped too!" I said.

Jenny gave me a funny look. "Nelson?"

"Mick's dog," I explained.

Jenny nodded. "I didn't know about Nelson," she said. "But he did always love dogs."

"When did you last see Mick?" I asked.

She wiped away a tear. "15 years ago," she said.

That was as long as I had been alive. As we went up two floors to Mick's ward, I thought about that. I couldn't imagine being without Dad for 15 days, never mind 15 years. It must have been horrible for her.

I had butterflies in my stomach as Dad went in to speak to Mick. I was so concerned that he would get angry. When Dad came out of the room, he looked worried.

"He's not angry," Dad said. "He didn't say much, to be honest."

I stood up. "Let me speak to him."

Uncle Jeff put his arm round me. "No, son," he said. "This is about Jenny and her dad."

"Please?"

Even though I could tell Jenny was worried, she still smiled. "You've done so much," she told me. "But I think I should talk to him. I'll tell you what happens – promise."

We waited for nearly an hour. When Jenny returned, she looked like she'd been crying. But then she smiled, and I realised it had gone OK.

"He told me he was scared of seeing me," she said. "He thought I hated him, but I don't.

Something just changed in him after Mum died. He was angry at the world and then I went off and he couldn't handle it. He said it was hard for him to accept that I'd married a black man." She wiped away more tears. "He told me that he wanted to call," she said. "But he took too long, and was ashamed. My kids got older and older, and he was convinced it was too late."

"But you're OK now?" I asked. "Like, it's all sorted?"

Jenny smiled. "It's a start. One step at a time, I guess."

Dad smiled too. "One step is all it takes, sometimes," he said.

Jenny looked at me. "All thanks to you," she said. "He called you a daft little shit. But in a nice way. I think he really likes you, Harvey."

"He's a daft old shit," I said, feeling embarrassed.

"Yeah," Jenny said. "Yeah, he is."

ONE MONTH LATER ...

My dad hired two men to mend Mick's fence. I sat on the grass with Amelia and Nelson and watched them work. Then, all of a sudden, the dog sat up and started to bark. It was his happy bark. I heard someone opening Mick's back door. There was Mick and Jenny! Mick looked so much better, but he was still unsteady on his feet.

"Mick!" I shouted in delight.

"Harvey," he said. "What you doing to my garden?"

Nelson bounded over and started to lick Mick's hand. Mick reached across and patted Nelson's head.

"Dad paid for it," I said. "Didn't think you'd mind."

Mick eyed the workmen and the new fence panels. Then he also clocked that his garden had been cleared. In place of the weeds and broken flowerpots, we'd planted shrubs and flowers.

Mum had also replaced the broken glass in his greenhouse.

I introduced him to Amelia and Mick took her hand. "You and that nosy git saved my life," he said to her. "Thank you."

Amelia blushed and told him it was OK. Then Jenny thanked her and they started chatting.

"You never found my budgie in the end, did you?" Mick said to me.

I grinned. "Nah," I replied. "We made budgie tikka masala with it. Tasty ..."

"You daft sod," he said.

Then he looked at the fence again. "Can you ask your dad to come out?" he asked, his face serious.

"Hey Mick," Dad said, when I brought him out.

"Is this your idea?" Mick asked, and he pointed at the fence.

Dad nodded. "Looks good, doesn't it?"

Mick shook his head. "No, Mr Singh, it doesn't."

I felt my stomach sink. Was the nasty Mick back, even after everything we'd been through? Mick walked slowly towards the new fence. He stopped at the spot where the big gap had been. The fence posts were up but the panel hadn't gone in yet.

"This bit here," he said. "I don't like it."

My dad looked puzzled. "But it's a brand new fence, Mick," he said.

Mick nodded. "Thing is," he said. "If you put this panel back, Nelson won't be able to come into your garden."

I saw Mick grin and I smiled too. Nelson barked and wagged his tail.

"And I won't be able to follow him ..." Mick added.

That was when I realised that you could teach an old dog, new tricks. Or an old Mick even ...

Our books are tested
for children and young people by
children and young people.

Thanks to everyone who consulted on
a manuscript for their time and effort in
helping us to make our books better
for our readers.